How Winston Delivered Christmas

*For Winston and his mummy and daddy, Sarah and Simon.
You can't make old friends. X*

First published 2018 by Macmillan Children's Books

This edition published 2021 by Macmillan Children's Books
an imprint of Pan Macmillan
The Smithson, 6-9 Briset Street, London, EC1M 5NR
EU representative: Macmillan Publishers Ireland Ltd, 1st Floor,
The Liffey Trust Centre, 117–126 Sheriff Street Upper
Dublin 1, D01 YC43
Associated companies throughout the world
www.panmacmillan.com

Copyright © Alex T. Smith 2018
ISBN 978-1-5290-8085-8

1 3 5 7 9 8 6 4 2

A CIP catalogue record for this book is available from the British Library.

Design by Alison Still

Printed and bound in CPI Group (UK) Ltd, Croydon CR0 4YY

MIX
Paper from
responsible sources
FSC® C116313
www.fsc.org

HOW WINSTON DELIVERED CHRISTMAS

Alex T. Smith

MACMILLAN CHILDREN'S BOOKS

How Winston Delivered Christmas is a book written in 24½ chapters. You can read it as quickly as you want to (maybe even gobble it all up in one go!) or you can start reading it on the 1st of December, and then read one chapter a day in the run-up to the 25th, finishing with the ½ chapter at the end on Christmas Day itself. It could be fun to get cosy and read the story all by yourself, or you could share it with a grown-up. Maybe have a biscuit at the same time. Books and biscuits go so nicely together, I think.

Alex T. Smith

CONTENTS

A VERY
IMPORTANT
MISSION

The toy shop on Mistletoe Street was crowded and noisy.

There were exactly twelve minutes left before it was supposed to close for the holidays, but people were

still shuffling in through the door hoping to pick up just one last present for a special someone, or to gawp at all the jolly toys sitting smartly on the shelves and admire the enormous doll's house in the window.

One person not looking at any of that was Oliver. His mum and dad owned the shop. He had been helping them all day – fetching and carrying and generally being very busy indeed. But now he quickly ducked out from under the counter where he'd been wrapping parcels. He flung his scarf around his neck and wiggled his way through the crowds and out into the busy high street.

He was on a VERY important mission.

It was late afternoon, the moon was

already up and snow had started to fall. Hundreds of snowflakes twirled through the air like ballerinas before landing daintily on the blanket of snow that had fallen over the past few days.

Oliver crunched down the street. He rushed past the bakery and the butcher's shop, sidestepped customers spilling out of the general store and the cheesemonger's, and swerved neatly around the ladies bustling out of the shop that sold fancy hats and ribbons. The entire night fizzed with Christmassy excitement.

On the corner of the street a brass band was standing in the cold, filling the evening air with a jazzy, parpy rendition of Oliver's favourite Christmas song.

He stopped and listened for a
moment before remembering his mission.
He weaved his way around the final
knot of shoppers (their arms piled high
with boxes and bags) and stopped in front
of a bright red letterbox.
He rummaged in
his pockets.

They were full, as usual, with all the Extremely Important Things you need to have on your person when you are eight years old:

- A couple of paperclips (twisted open into wiggly strips of metal).
- Some string tangled up into several useless knots.
- The stub of a blunt pencil.
- Fluff.
- And a dry wrinkled old conker collected in October.

All of this was Vital.

Eventually Oliver found what he was actually looking for – an envelope. It wasn't too badly crumpled and he'd written the address on the front in

his very best handwriting. He'd left it a bit late to send but he crossed his fingers and hoped it would get where it needed to go in time.

He was just about to put it in the slot on the letterbox when someone called his name.

'Oliver! Oliver?'

It was his mum. She was standing in the doorway of their shop, waving at him.

'Hurry up! I need your help wrapping these last few teddy bears!' she cried. 'And it's much too cold to be outside without your coat on!'

'Coming!' called Oliver, waving back.

He quickly popped his letter in the box and scurried back down the street into the busy shop.

Now whether Oliver's envelope got caught up in the chilly breeze or was found by a shimmer of winter magic that was fizzing about that night nobody knows, but the letter didn't stay in the letterbox for long. When no one was looking, it slid back out and danced through the air and down the street, floating along between the snowflakes.

A MYSTERIOUS
FLYING OBJECT

A short while later when the shops had all eventually closed, a small grubby white mouse poked his nose out from under the pile of rubbish he had been rummaging in. He was in a dark alleyway, going through the bins trying to find something to eat and something he could wrap himself up in for the night, but he wasn't having much luck. Newspapers usually made good blankets but all the pieces he could find tonight had been snowed on so were now soggy and not very cosy at all.

He looked around a bit more. *Oh! This looks more likely!* he thought. He'd found a piece of soft fabric poking out from under the snow. He gave it a good heave but it turned out to be much smaller and not quite as stuck as he'd anticipated and he flew backwards and landed on his bottom with a bump. He shook his ears and took a proper look at the fabric. It wasn't large enough for him to use as a blanket. It was just a thin strip of tweed that had been thrown out by the man in the tailor shop nearby.

The little mouse sighed. 'Never mind, Winston,' he squeaked to himself. 'You can use it as a scarf!' And he wrapped it around his neck.

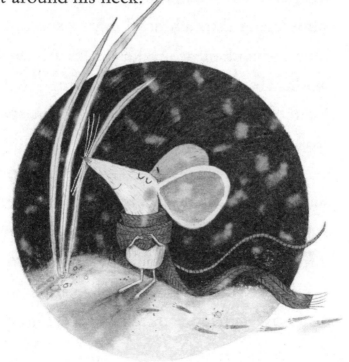

Well, it certainly kept that little bit of him a touch warmer but it didn't do much for the rest of him. The night was bitterly cold and he was shivering from the top of his ears to the tip of his tail.

Winston decided to have a rest for a moment. When you are very tiny, rummaging through anything – especially human-sized bins – takes a lot of hard work. He found the driest corner of a cardboard box, settled himself down and closed his eyes.

Winston took a big sniff. All around him, the evening air was filled with the smell of dinners being taken out of ovens and party food being laid out on silver trays in the houses and hotels nearby.

He sniffed again. He could smell

roast potatoes and tiny fancy canapés, fresh bread and cheeses of all levels of delicious stinkiness.

There was a little tickle of treacle pudding on the air and a whiff of jam roly-poly pudding so good that Winston wanted to roll himself up in it.

His stomach groaned and so did he. None of that food would find its way to his tummy. He needed to find something that he could nibble on now and more importantly somewhere warm and dry(ish) to sleep. But where? He'd looked everywhere in those bins and there was nothing useful or edible in any of them. He'd have to try elsewhere.

He stood up and shook the fresh snow from the top of his ears. He was just about to clamber down from his perch when he heard a whooshing sort of sound coming from behind him. He turned around to see what it was – *Probably a pigeon looking for something to eat too*, he thought – but saw instead a flat brownish object flying straight towards him! Before he could wiggle a whisker the object crashed into him, sending him flying through the air, and he landed head first in the freezing cold snow.

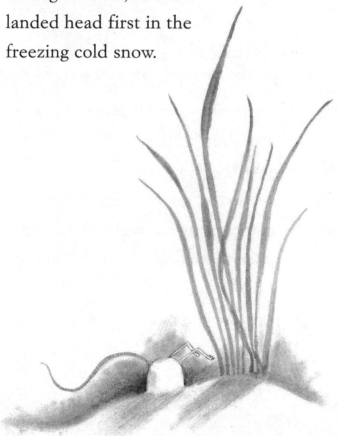

AN ENVELOPE
OUT OF PLACE

It took a few moments for Winston to turn himself up the right way and untangle his tail. He dusted himself down and rubbed his nose. *What just happened?* he wondered. What WAS that thing that had knocked him over?

He clambered back up the snow-covered pile of rubbish and looked around to find who, or what, the culprit was. It didn't take him long to find it and his heart skipped a beat. It was an envelope. Winston couldn't believe his luck! Now for most people an ordinary envelope isn't something to get terribly excited about, but for Winston this was a real treat. Of all the things to find on a very cold winter's night like tonight an envelope – and a dryish one at that – was brilliant! He'd be able to rip a little hole in it and wiggle inside for the night. It would be like a nice papery sleeping bag that would keep him lovely and snug and out of the wind and snow.

Winston sprang across the bins in several zingy leaps and picked it up. He was just about to tear a tiny hole in the side of it when something stopped him. He wasn't sure what it was but something made his nose twitch and his whiskers tingle. He found himself turning the envelope around so he could read the writing on the front.

For a mouse, Winston was very good at reading. When your bed is usually made from bits of newspaper it's inevitable that you end up working out what all the black marks on the paper mean just to entertain yourself. Besides, getting a library card can be quite tricky when you are a mouse.

Winston ran his paw across the neat handwriting. It said:

To Father Christmas
Mince Pie House
Just Past That Snowdrift
The North Pole
URGENT!

He gasped.
This wasn't any ordinary envelope –

it was addressed to Father Christmas! That must mean that the letter inside was very important. But what on earth was it doing floating about and knocking little mice off their feet? Surely it should be sitting in a neat pile in Father Christmas's warm, cosy workshop right now?

It must have got mislaid when the postman was emptying the letterbox, he thought. And, as much as he really wanted to snuggle inside the envelope and get warm, he knew he couldn't possibly do that. This letter needed to get to Father Christmas!

'I'll take it to the letterbox and post it so that it can get to the North Pole in time for Christmas Eve,' Winston said to himself. But even as the words squeaked out of his mouth, he felt that something wasn't adding up. He counted the days off on his paws to try to work out what day, or rather – night, it actually was. When that didn't work (mice aren't brilliant with numbers) he quickly rummaged through the rubbish pile near him until he found the scrap of newspaper he'd uncovered earlier. It was from yesterday's edition – Winston knew that because he'd slept under another scrap of it the night before.

He turned it the right way up and unfolded the soggy corner. 'Uh oh . . .' said Winston. The newspaper was dated the 23rd of December, which meant today was the 24th, and THAT meant that it was already Christmas Eve!

WINSTON
SETS OFF

Goodness! There wasn't a moment to lose! If he was going to get this letter to the North Pole he'd have to get going straight away!

Winston had never experienced Christmas before, but he knew all about Father Christmas. Over the past few weeks the entire world had gone Christmas-mad. The shops were packed to the rafters from morning to night with busy-looking people bustling about with long lists and their arms full of boxes and parcels. Winston had watched bemused. What was it all about? Who was this jolly man with the beard and the smart red suit whose picture seemed to be appearing everywhere?

Then one night about a week ago Winston had found quite a good place to sleep. It was a small den near the basement kitchen window of one of the grander houses in the city. Spots like this were always good places to spend a night but unfortunately you couldn't stop there for long – cooks didn't tend to like mice hanging around their kitchens. Luckily no one had noticed Winston so he enjoyed the lovely food smells that had floated out of the open window and the great wafts of heat that rolled out every time the oven doors had been opened.

Later in the evening when Winston had been thinking about going to sleep, the cook and the butler had rolled up their sleeves to get stuck into the piles of

washing up and had popped the radio on to keep them company. Winston had been enthralled. There'd been lovely Christmas music, choirs singing and a lot of talk about Father Christmas. Apparently on Christmas Eve this Father Christmas person put on his nice warm coat and hat and set off on a sleigh pulled by flying reindeer from the North Pole. He delivered presents to every child across the world. And all before morning!

How exciting! Winston thought. And how nice it would be to have a little fireplace all of his own on which to hang up a stocking. Now standing in the alleyway, Winston sighed at the idea of it. Then he thought of the poor child whose letter hadn't made it to Father

Christmas's house. They would wake up in the morning to find no presents in their stocking or hidden under the Christmas tree.

Winston wrapped his tatty scarf neatly around his neck again and tried to ignore the grumbling, rumbling noises coming from his tummy. This was an extremely important job.

He picked up the envelope and marched very decisively to the end of the alleyway and out into the street.

Then he stopped.

Where exactly IS the North Pole? he wondered. He knew it was north but quite *how* far north was it? His legs were only very small and the snow made it rather difficult to travel very quickly – especially lugging a letter with him all the way. He'd probably only have a few hours to get there, so he'd have to make sure he was going in the right direction.

All around him, people were still rushing and there were legs striding about in all directions. Tired legs belonging to commuters heading home after work; excited legs of people going out to Christmas Eve parties; and giddy little legs, mainly belonging to the smaller human beings who were running around hooting and hollering and messing about in the snow.

All of this was quite confusing for Winston who felt very tiny indeed.

'What I need,' Winston squeaked to himself, 'is a map.'

But where could a mouse find one of those on Christmas Eve? The bookshops were closed and even the museum, which Winston knew had a great collection of very old maps, was shut until after the holidays.

Just then an idea landed rather neatly in Winston's mind. There was a shop not far away from where he was – *On Mistletoe Street*, he thought – that might be able to help him.

Tucking the envelope under his arm, Winston set off.

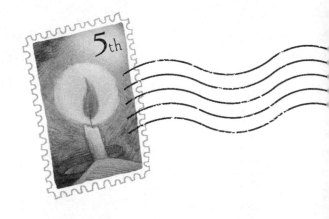

WINDOW
SHOPPING

The shops on Mistletoe Street had closed their doors for the evening but there was still plenty going on. People were strolling about and the band on the corner was playing jolly Christmas music with such parpy and

tooting enthusiasm that it made Winston's tiny toes tap and his heart bounce to the beat as he crunched through the snow with the letter.

The street was looking particularly lovely tonight.

It was one of the oldest streets in the city – a hodgepodge of buildings all cobbled together so tightly and in such a ramshackle way that you felt that with just one strong gust of wind they could all topple over like dominoes.

Tonight it looked more magical than ever, as if a giant baker had made the buildings out of huge slabs of gingerbread and sprinkled them with icing sugar. With the snowflakes falling and the ropes of twinkling lights strung amongst the bare winter trees, it was like a picture on the front of a chocolate box.

Winston knew he had to be quick but he couldn't help having just the tiniest nosy in the shop windows as he walked by.

First, unfortunately for Winston's rumbling stomach, was the bakery. It was a three-storey building that grew narrower with each floor so that it looked like a three-tiered wedding cake. Winston looked dreamily at all the cakes and treats displayed in the enormous window at the front of the store. There were large Christmas cakes covered with gleaming white icing as smooth as a frozen pond. Some were decorated with Christmas-tree biscuits, and one cake had a large edible snowman sitting on top of it!

Dancing around the cakes were gingerbread men and women. Winston knew they were only made from dough but he wished he could slip through the window and dance with them. The centrepiece of the display was an enormous gingerbread castle, golden brown and dusted with sugar. Shiny boiled sweets had been melted down to make the windows so that a light shining from inside made them look like real stained glass glinting in the moonlight. Winston's tummy growled loudly at the smells – marzipan, ginger, plump soaked cherries and perfectly baked cakes – which wafted temptingly from the gap under the door. (It was just too narrow for him

to squeeze under . . .)

Reluctantly he turned and kept going down the street.

He passed the haberdasher's with the dressmaker's dummies standing in the window modelling snazzy outfits perfect for the cold winter weather. There were bolts of fabric propped up behind them and a collection of pretty sewing baskets overflowing with shiny buttons and trimmings.

Winston had become quite attached to the tatty scarf he was wearing but he decided that a little coat made out of the cosy blue velvet on display would really look quite lovely on him and keep him snug too!

He scampered on. Next came the sweet shop with its enormous glass jars filled with all manner of delicious-looking treats and, in the middle of the display, a fat little fir tree covered with candy canes. Winston thought it looked so pretty with its confectionery decorations, even if he wasn't completely sure why there was a tree INSIDE the shop.

An icy blast of air suddenly shivered down Mistletoe Street. It took Winston rather by surprise and made his ears blow inside out. As he struggled to fix them the envelope in his paws escaped and danced off down the street.

He squeaked and raced after it. With a well-judged leap he dived on it and, after a few roly-poly tumbles, he and the letter skidded to a stop outside another brightly lit shop. Winston dusted himself down and glanced up at the window. He stopped dead in his tracks and gasped.

He couldn't believe what he was looking at.

THE ROOM IN
THE RAFTERS

It was BEAUTIFUL.

Winston was outside a toy shop and the golden glow from inside illuminated the snowy pavement around him. The window had been carefully designed so that it looked like a miniature version of Mistletoe Street. Little toy-sized shops were set up and covered in pretend snow. Beautiful dolls and teddy bears were busily going about their Christmassy business. Miniature trees were covered in twinkly lights and a little band of wind-up figures was playing a song on their tiny tin instruments. Behind the street a toy train chugged and puffed real smoke as it made its way back and forth across the window and a beautifully carved fairground wheel, complete with plush animal passengers, turned in time to the band's music.

All of this was wonderful, but what Winston couldn't pull his eyes away from was the towering doll's house in the middle of the scene. The front had been opened up so that you could peek at its five floors. Each room had been carefully decorated. Winston stood with his nose pressed against the glass.

Through the front door there was a hallway with a beautifully tiled floor and lamps that flickered warmly. A collection of tiny coats was hanging on a coat stand, and some Wellington boots no bigger than thimbles were drying on miniature sheets of newspaper.

On the floor below a busy kitchen scene was being played out. Little saucepans bubbled and quivered on the stoves, and every so often puffs of steam escaped from the glowing ovens. Course after course of beautiful food was cooking away ready for the party that was taking

place upstairs in the dining room. This was a grand room with ornate wallpaper and a large (for a doll's house) chandelier sparkling above the long table.

Winston's eyes wandered to the comfortable drawing room where – Winston gasped – every wall was lined with tiny books. A plump armchair with a comfy cushion and a footstool was set in front

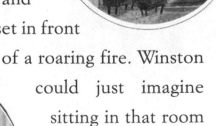

of a roaring fire. Winston could just imagine sitting in that room

after dinner with a blanket over his knees, having a nice little nap with a full belly.

Upstairs was a grand bedroom, a bathroom with a deep bath (with real bubbles floating about) and a nursery with tiny toys and even its own doll's house!

He looked up to the final floor and sighed so deeply that a blossom of hot air momentarily fogged up the glass in front of him. He wiped it away with his

paw and his eyes gleamed.

Tucked away under the sloping roof was the cosiest-looking little room Winston had ever seen. It wasn't as grand or as elegant as some of the other rooms on the floors below but to Winston it looked like the snuggliest, most beautiful room ever. There was an overflowing bookcase full of titchy books and the cosy bed was piled high with pillows, soft blankets and even a little patchwork quilt. A lamp was glowing softly beside the bed next to a mug of steaming cocoa. Everything was perfectly to scale and just right for a doll . . .

Or a mouse, thought Winston.

How lovely it would be to live in such a place! And how exciting it

would be for any boy or girl to find a doll's house like this in the morning, all wrapped up with a big bow tied around the middle.

Winston sighed again. Just imagining that scene made him feel warm from the tips of his ears to the bottom of his paws. This doll's house would make such a special present for someone.

Present . . . Christmas . . . Christmas present . . .

Winston shook himself. What on earth was he doing standing here gawping in shop windows when he had a job to do? Time was ticking away! If he didn't hurry, the letter-writer wouldn't get any presents at all. With a final glance at the attic room, he scampered off to find out exactly where the North Pole actually was.

THE JOLLY
HOLIDAY
TRAVEL AGENTS

The shop Winston had actually been looking for was a little further down the road where Mistletoe Street turned and all the buildings started to wiggle down a bit of a hill. It was a small, skinny shop that was wedged between a pie shop (the smell of warm pastry wafting out from under the front door was almost too much for Winston) and a wool shop (which had a funny display in the window of clockwork sheep in snazzy woollen jumpers leaping over knitted parcels).

But what Winston was most interested in now stood before him. He read the words painted above the window carefully.

. . . and underneath:

Say Bonjour! Ciao! ¡Hola! Hej Hej!
to the Whole Wide World!

Yes, this was definitely the place Winston needed if he was going to find out exactly where the North Pole was and how best to get there.

Winston scampered closer and peered carefully at all the photographs that were hanging in the window. Each one was different and as Winston studied them he tried to remember everything he had heard about the North Pole on the radio. It was apparently very, very cold and snowy. Father Christmas's only neighbours would be polar bears!

Winston could feel a nervous wiggly-jiggly sort of feeling starting to flutter in his tummy. None of the pictures showed anywhere that looked right. All the photographs were of hot, sunny places.

There were photos of boats sailing past sandy beaches and pictures of cities full of towering buildings that reached up into the sky. There was no snow anywhere.

What am I going to do? he thought to himself. His cheeks were glowing red as a little wave of worry started to rise from the tips of his toes all the way up to his ears.

He noticed that each of the pictures had a thin strand of gold thread attached to it which stretched across the window to a large model globe in the middle of the scene. The threads showed you where each of the exotic places shown in the pictures was located on the globe.

Winston was just thinking that none of that helped him very much when he noticed two white patches on the globe.

One at the bottom and one at the top. *White*, Winston thought. Like the snow all around him.

'I wonder . . .' he squeaked to himself and a little burst of excitement went off in his chest like a firework.

He dashed over to the drainpipe and stashed the envelope carefully behind it. Then he clambered up the metal pipe and, wiggling just for a second to judge the distance right, leaped on to the window ledge. When he got to the middle he wiped away the little patch of fog caused by his breath and peered in at the globe. The splodge of white at the bottom said 'Antarctica' and, under that, 'South Pole'. Winston's nose waggled excitedly. If the South Pole was at the bottom he would bet his whiskers on the other patch of white being the North Pole! Of course he thought he'd better just check.

With a nimble leap Winston managed to jump up and grab hold of the leading between the panes of glass. He pulled himself upon to it, wobbling slightly as there wasn't really enough room for him to stand properly. With another leap and a heave he was standing on the next length of leading where he was able to look down on to the globe.

'Yippee!' squeaked Winston when his eyes had darted across the white continent and seen what was written there: 'The Arctic' . . . and the 'North Pole'! He'd found it!

But his excitement was short lived.

It was an awfully long way away. A very long way away indeed. How would he, with his tiny paws, travel all that distance before midnight?

His brain was racing. He was trying to think of a solution to this problem when he heard a noise coming from behind him. His body stiffened against the glass and his ears twitched nervously.

Then a loud voice said, 'WHAT ON EARTH DO YOU THINK YOU ARE DOING?'

Winston was so surprised that his little feet slipped this way and that along the icy window leading. His tiny arms windmilled wildly as he tried to balance and his paws grabbed madly at the glass. But it was no use. With a loud startled squeak

Winston slipped and
found himself falling
backwards through the
chilly air and landed
ears-deep in the snow below.

THINKING BIG
THOUGHTS

Oh bother! thought Winston glumly from upside down and tummy-deep in a snowdrift.

Then he felt a tight pinch on the end of his tail and found himself being plucked free from the snow. A shiver of dread shimmied down his whole body and he squeezed his eyes tightly shut so he couldn't see who or what was pulling him free.

I'm probably going to be gobbled up! He panicked.

But no gobbling came.

Not even a nibble.

Instead he was placed carefully on the ground. After a few seconds he decided to be brave and peek through his eyelashes.

'Oh!' he squeaked, opening his eyes wide.

What was standing in front of him wasn't a monster about to eat him up – but a pigeon. A big, plump pigeon who was looking at him with her head tilted to one side.

'Oh good!' she cooed. 'You're OK! I was ever so worried for a moment. I didn't mean to startle you and make you fall but we were sitting up there –' she flapped a wing in the general direction of a bare winter tree – 'and I said to myself, "Now, what's going on there, Edna?"– I'm Edna, by the way – and I saw you start to climb up those windows, and I said, "There's going to be a terrible accident in a minute," what with you being so tiny and climbing so high and those windows in this weather can be very slippy. So I said to myself, "I'm going to go and see what's happening!" Didn't I, George? George!'

Edna squinted up at the tree again.

'Oh!' she eventually continued. 'He's still up there.' Then she squawked 'GEORGE!', so loudly that Winston almost found himself knocked off his feet again.

A couple of seconds later a sleepy and slightly grumpy voice came from the heights of the tree, accompanied by some fluttering.

'All right! I'm on my way! Keep your feathers on!'

A short moment later a robin landed next to Winston. Well, he thought it was a robin because it had lovely red feathers on its chest. But it was so plump it looked like a small, feathery tennis ball with a beak and two tiny stick legs coming out of the bottom of it.

'This is George,' said Edna.

'I'm George,' George yawned.

'As I was saying,' continued Edna, 'we saw you and wondered what on earth you were up to! It's Christmas Eve – you should be tucked up asleep somewhere cosy.'

'Well, yes . . .' said Winston. 'But, you see, I have a Very Important Job to do tonight!'

He dashed over to fetch the envelope and showed it to Edna and George.

He explained all about how he'd found it and that he needed to deliver it to Father Christmas at the North Pole before midnight.

'That's when he sets off to deliver all the Christmas presents across the world,'

Winston said. He glanced back up at the travel agent's window and sighed. 'But the North Pole is an awfully long way from here. According to that globe up there it's across an ocean and I don't think I'll be able to find a boat to get me there in time. It's already getting quite late . . .'

Saying that out loud suddenly made Winston feel very sad and disappointed. If the envelope didn't get there whoever had written the letter wouldn't have a very happy Christmas the next day.

Edna saw Winston's whiskers wobble and his ears go a bit floppy. He looked so forlorn and droopy. *Well*, she thought. *That just won't do.*

'Now,' she said, 'let's not get ourselves down in the dumps! Every problem has a solution, doesn't it, George?'

George, who had been having forty-winks leaning against Edna, started then quickly agreed with her. 'Oh yes!' he said. 'A solution!'

Edna wandered around in a circle thinking Big Thoughts, then let out an excited squawk! 'Oh! How silly I've been!' she cried, fluffing herself up. 'Follow me!' And, with that, she started to stalk very briskly down Mistletoe Street.

Winston looked at George and George looked at Winston. They didn't know what was happening but they realized that the best thing would be to do as she said. Winston tucked the envelope under his arm again then he and George

started off down the street after their friend.

'Are we going to the North Pole?' Winston panted as he scampered behind Edna.

'No!' cooed Edna, without slowing down. 'No need to go there my dear – I'm pretty sure that Father Christmas is already here in the city!'

MINCE PIES
AND MOVIES

Winston didn't have a chance to ask any more questions as it was all he and George could do to try and keep up with Edna. She was waddling and fluttering as fast as she could down Mistletoe Street and around the corner on to the large, busy road that cut a long, wiggly line through the city.

'I'm confused!' Winston panted. 'How can Father Christmas be here? He should be in the North Pole getting himself ready to set off.'

'Aha!' cried Edna. '*Should* be. But what if he isn't? When you said about him being in the North Pole this evening, I thought, *That's strange*, but didn't know why . . . Then I remembered! He couldn't be in the North Pole because I'd seen him earlier. We both had, hadn't we, George?'

George didn't reply because he was too busy huffing and puffing and wafting his hot face with one of his wings.

It didn't stop Edna though. She carried on talking.

'Me and George don't fly about as much as we used to, do we, dear? Not at our age. But one thing we do like to do is go to the Empire, don't we, George?'

George had just about got his breath back enough to say, 'Yes, the Empire.'

'What's that?' asked Winston, feeling bamboozled.

'It's a moving-picture house. You know: movies! Talkies! The flicks! When the ticket man isn't looking we sneak in! It's nice and warm in there and so dark nobody notices you. There's a bakery next door and we have a good feast on all the broken biscuits and cake crumbs out the back, then in we go to the cinema. I like looking at the pictures and George likes having a nice nap in the warm, don't you, dear?'

George was asleep again.

Winston had no idea what any of this had to do with Father Christmas and the North Pole but he carried on listening as best he could. Edna had paused for breath and to get her bearings.

'Yes – this way!' she cried, and started waddling and fluttering down the road again.

Winston hurried after her, followed by George, who may or may not have been actually sleepwalking.

'We went there this morning and

that's where I saw him – Father Christmas!' Edna continued.

'At the movies?' asked Winston, his eyes like saucers.

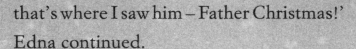

'No,' said Edna. 'Outside. And with any luck he'll still be there!'

As she said that she rounded a corner with Winston and George still tagging along behind her. They were now at a very busy intersection where several roads all came together.

All around them were cinemas and restaurants and shops and theatres. Lots of people were milling about and bright lights glittered everywhere. Winston spotted the Empire cinema building with its name written in huge letters all picked out with electric light bulbs.

'Aha!' hooted Edna all of a sudden. She sounded very pleased with herself. 'There he is!'

Winston squinted. He could see lots of people, but none of them were dressed in red with a big, fluffy white beard. 'Where?'

Edna grinned beakily.

'Look up!' she cooed.

AN IMPORTANT CLUE

Winston craned his neck to see what Edna was pointing at.

Attached to the side of one of the large buildings overlooking the busy traffic roundabout were lots of enormous signs advertising various things: theatres, cinemas, chocolate bars and even expensive snazzy socks. Some of the signs were completely lit up; others had light bulbs all around them flashing on and off at different intervals; some had words picked out in fancy light-up writing which fizzed and flickered brightly against the dark night sky.

In the middle of all this was what Edna had wanted to show Winston. On a huge advertising board, which must have been at least twenty feet high, was the smiling, jolly face of Father Christmas! It was definitely him! He had the white fluffy beard, happy twinkly eyes and the red velvet suit that looked very warm and cosy.

Winston's heart lifted. Then it

BUTTERWORTHS

RICH & DELICIOUS

CHOCOLATE

EST. 1847

FORTESQUES

—DEPARTMENT—
STORE

Visit Father
Christmas
in store
today!

Sunbeam
TONIC

will perk
you UP!

CAFÉ

THE EMPIRE CINEMA

DAUB &
SPATTER

Fine Art
Supplies

Good
Boy
Dog
Food

It's Woof-ly

TOASTY
TOES

LUXURY SOCKS
for
DISCERNING FEET

BELLE MAIN

HAND LOTION

for the softest hands

STORIES FOR
ALL IMAGINATIONS
S.R. THOMAS & Co.
BOOK STORE

EST. 1847

FORTESQUES

— DEPARTMENT — STORE

Visit Father Christmas in store today!

plummeted again. This wasn't the real Father Christmas. It was just a nice picture of him in an advert. Winston said this sadly to Edna.

Edna chuckled. 'Oh, you are a silly mouse!' she said kindly. 'Of course it's just a picture. But I think it might also be a clue as to where you can actually find him here in the city. Have a read of the sign!'

Winston looked up again and squinted his eyes against the snow that was still falling all around him. The sign said:

FORTESQUE'S
DEPARTMENT STORE
Visit Father Christmas in store today!

Winston's cheeks went pink with excitement. Could it be true? Could Father Christmas really be here in the city? He had to find out! He didn't really know what a department store was but it sounded exciting. Perhaps it was somewhere Father Christmas went to get the supplies he'd need for his long journey around the world? He'd surely need at least a couple of packets of biscuits to keep him going for the night . . .

'Do you know where Fortesque's Department Store is, Edna?' Winston asked, quivering with excitement.

Edna walked around in a little circle while she thought.

'I don't think it's very far from here. You'll need to cross this road VERY

CAREFULLY and then just take that big road there and keep going straight down until you get to the shop. If I remember rightly, it's quite a big one with its name in large letters above the door.'

'Will you both come with me?' asked Winston. He'd got quite used to having a nice friend or two with him now. It made him stop thinking about how cold his paws were and how grumbly his stomach was.

'Oh, I wish I could, my dear,' said Edna. 'I love an adventure but I've got to get poor George back to our nest. Look at him!'

Winston looked around and laughed. George was flat on his back with his two stick-like legs poking up in the air and he was snoring so loudly it sounded like an engine.

'This is what a belly full of mince pies does to you!' Edna chuckled as she pecked gently at George's tail to wake him up.

'Now you just continue on your adventure,' she said, turning to Winston. 'You seem a very brave sort of mouse and I know you can get that letter to Father Christmas before midnight! Be very careful – and good luck!'

Winston said thank you and let Edna fuss about wrapping his scrappy little scarf warmly around his neck with her beak.

Then with a little wave over his shoulder to the two birds he picked

up the envelope and set off towards
Fortesque's Department Store to meet
Father Christmas himself!

To Father Christmas
Mince Pie House
...t .... That Snowdrift
The ...

A COSY BED
MADE OF
STRAW

Winston was on his way. He was feeling a jumble of excitement and nerves. He was excited because it seemed as if his task of delivering his letter to Father Christmas would be accomplished much quicker and with less travelling-over-an-ocean than he thought. But he was also nervous because he was now in the busiest part of the city.

All around him was noise and movement and flashing lights. Trams rattled down the centre of the wide road and there were many lanes of honking, hooting and sputtering automobiles whizzing past. Far below his paws Winston could feel the underground trains rumbling and grumbling.

He weaved his way through the crowds of people on the pavement. Many of them looked like they were on their way to parties. Women in long gowns that sparkled in the headlights of the passing vehicles picked their way along the pavement on fancy high-heeled shoes.

(Winston had to be very careful of those!) There were men in shiny two-tone shoes and when Winston looked up at them he saw they were all wearing smart suits with snazzy bow ties.

As Winston made his way through these glamorous people he stopped feeling nervous and started to feel very Christmassy.

'I'll deliver this letter to Father Christmas,' he squeaked to himself. 'Then I'll find somewhere snuggly to spend the night and have a good sleep – I'll need it after all this adventuring!'

Suddenly he heard something unusual. It was music but not like the loud jazzy music that had been floating out of the restaurants and clubs he'd just scurried past. This was gentle, like a lullaby. Winston stopped to listen for a moment, his ears waggling like antennae trying to find out where it was coming from. He followed the sound and found it was coming from an old building with a tall pointy tower that was set slightly back from the main road. A soft, warm, flickering light was coming from within and Winston sneaked in through a gap in the door.

The inside of the building was beautiful and Winston was transfixed by the carved ceiling and colourful stained-glass windows. Hundreds of candles flickered softly making the whole place feel very peaceful. He wasn't alone. The building was full of people sitting on long benches listening quietly to a choir at the front singing beautiful music. Winston knew some of the words because he'd heard them being played on the radio and by bands in the city. *Christmas carols*, he thought.

As he looked around he spotted a curious object set up nearby. It was a large toy building a bit like a doll's house but it looked more like a barn or a stable. Inside several statues were standing on a bed of clean, sweet-smelling straw. There was a woman in blue and several men. Some were dressed in fancy clothes and others were dressed like farmers and there were even some pretend sheep standing beside them. Everyone was looking at a tiny wooden box in the middle. It was filled with straw and inside, fast asleep, was a tiny model baby.

That does look like a nice place to have a sleep, Winston thought, and he yawned. Perhaps it wouldn't hurt if he just had the tiniest of naps there beside the baby? But as he began clambering into the stable scene the choir finished singing and the congregation clapped. The sudden noise made Winston stop sharply in his tracks. He waggled his whiskers.

'Winston!' he said sternly to himself. 'Fancy thinking about having a nap when you haven't finished your Important Job!' And with a flick of his tail he forced himself to pad down the aisle and back out into the cold night. He thought about the little baby asleep in the wooden box full of straw and promised himself that, as it was Christmas Eve, he would come back when the letter was delivered and have a nap in that nice peaceful building while candles flickered warmly around him.

SPLASH AND
SPLATTER!

Winston continued scampering down the road to Fortesque's as fast as he could. His breath billowed out in front of him in great plumes of warm fog. He imagined for a moment that he was one of the enormous

trains that huffed and puffed in and out of the city from the busy stations dotted around town. His feet pitter-pattered along the pavement and, with his important letter tucked under his arm, Winston felt a bit giddy knowing that his mission would soon be completed.

He noticed that some of the people he passed were carrying parcels wrapped up in the jazziest paper, many of which were adorned with ribbons and crinkly bows. He wondered what could be inside the packages? What surprises lay inside for the recipients when they ripped off the paper in the morning?

Winston waggled his ears with excitement. With any luck, if he did his job right, the writer of the letter he was carrying would be waking up to similarly dressed parcels in the morning because he, Winston, had done a good job.

Unfortunately Winston's excitement didn't last long. As he pattered along the pavement thinking about silk ribbons and sparkly paper a bus full of excited Christmassy people whizzed towards him. As it drew near, the driver accidentally steered just that little bit too close to the edge of the road where slushy, half-melted, muddy snow was lying in a big puddly mess.

The wheels threw a great splash of the icy snow water up in the air which then splatted across the pavement. Most of the people managed to hop out of the way in time, but not Winston. The slush landed all over him. It was freezing cold and not one bit of him escaped it. He was coated from nose to tail in filthy, icy water.

Winston shook himself and wiped his eyes with the back of a paw. Thankfully, because the letter he was carrying had been rolled up under his arm, it wasn't too splattered with muck. Winston unravelled it and gave it a good shake. But this was his big mistake. He heard another van whizzing along the street beside him. There was no way Winston was going to be splattered again, so he dived out of the way. But the envelope slipped out of his wet paws! It was lifted high into the air above him before being snatched by a chilly puff of wind.

'NO!' squeaked Winston. He leaped up to try to grab it, but it was too high. Horrified, all Winston could do was stand covered in dripping muddy puddle water and watch as the wind blew the letter into the road. It fluttered about, buffeted against the sides of vehicles and whipped off windscreens by busy wipers before slapping to a halt against the traffic-light pole in the middle of the street.

He had to get it back and the only way to do that was to cross the busy road and try to not get himself squished in the process!

Winston gulped.

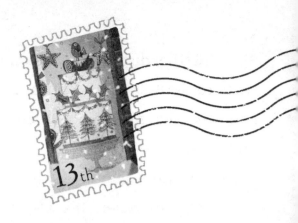

AS FLAT AS
A PANCAKE
(ALMOST)

'Come on, Winston,' he squeaked to himself. 'You can do this!'

But Winston didn't feel as if he could. The road was wide and very busy with traffic whizzing up and down it and the ground was slushy and slippery.

In the distance the letter was still stuck to the pole. The edges were twitching and wiggling as cars zoomed by but so far it hadn't flown off any further down the street into the oncoming vehicles.

Winston willed his whiskers to stop shivering.

He took a few steps forward so that his feet were right on the edge of the kerb. It WAS very dangerous for a tiny mouse like him to scamper into the road. He was too small for any of the drivers to see him and even more invisible against the swirling snow and bright, flashing headlights. As he watched the lights blurred together and shimmered like the chains of fairy lights that were wrapped and looped around the street lamps and trees on either side of the road. Normally he would have thought that it all looked rather pretty, but the only thing filling his mind at this moment was how big, wide and scary the space was between him and the letter.

He squeezed his eyes shut for a moment. 'You can do it!' he told himself again. 'You are a very brave mouse!'

And, he decided, *maybe this was true*. Usually at this time of night he would be tucked up in a hidey-hole somewhere trying to sleep and stay warm but tonight he'd already been doing lots of brave things. Winston braced himself. He was going to do it. He was going to retrieve the letter. Looking in the direction of the traffic, he spotted a small break in the line of vehicles and chose just that moment to leap off the kerb and dash part of the way across the road.

His heart was really pounding now.

He was stuck in the middle of two lanes of traffic. Cars whipped past him on both sides. The earth shuddered under his paws and great clouds of dirty black smoke coughed out from the exhaust pipes. Winston tried to focus on getting across the next bit of road and on to the small strip of raised pavement in the middle. He steeled himself, wiggled his nose and checked for a safe gap. He took a deep breath and scampered as quickly as he could across the slippery street. But he had misjudged the speed of the cars zooming down the road. It was disorientating.

A bus whizzed by and Winston spun around several times on the spot . . .

When he eventually managed to steady himself he didn't know where he'd come from or where he was meant to be going. He heard a loud roar behind him. He squeaked in alarm – an enormous car was heading straight for him! Its bright yellow headlights were blinding and they were getting nearer and nearer. If he didn't move he'd end up as flat as a pancake.

'WINSTON! MOVE!' he cried out to himself. But his tiny feet were frozen with fear. He crouched lower on the ground and put his paws over his head. He braced himself for a collision

with the car and closed his eyes tight.

He could feel the car coming closer.

And closer.

And closer.

14th

YOU AREN'T
A SALMON

All of a sudden, Winston felt himself being picked up gently by his tatty scarf and flung across the street on to the snowy pavement.

He landed heavily and rolled across the frozen ground. He just lay on the floor panting and willing his heart to stop thumping like a big bass drum. Without opening his eyes he patted himself down with his paws. He didn't feel as flat as a pancake, so what had happened?

He took a deep breath, opened his eyes and nearly fainted. Standing over him, with her face very close to his own, was a large, fluffy white cat! He panicked, squeaked in alarm and scrabbled backwards as quickly as he could, keeping his eyes on the feline fiend who was glaring at him.

But instead of pouncing on him the cat suddenly plonked herself down and lazily licked a paw.

'Darling, do come away from the edge of that road,' she drawled. 'I'm not going to rescue you again.'

Winston stopped scrabbling and scampered away from the kerb, making sure to keep the cat at an escape-able distance from him at all times.

'You r-rescued me?' stammered Winston.

The cat stopped grooming herself and looked at Winston.

'Of course!' she purred. 'You were about to be squished flat under the wheels of one of those cars. Very careless of you, I must say!'

When Winston didn't say anything, she continued: 'I live in one of the apartments near here. My people are

throwing a party this evening. Lots of nice party food and lovely music, but it got rather stuffy in there so I nipped out for some air. That's when I saw you from the other side of the road and could just *tell* you were about to get hit by one of these dreadful vehicles. Someone needed to help you because you weren't helping yourself.'

'And now you are going to eat me?' squeaked Winston in a small and terrified voice.

The cat looked mortally offended. 'EAT you?' she cried. 'Now why on earth would I eat a mouse?'

'Because that's what cats do, isn't it?' said Winston quietly. 'Eat mice . . .'

The cat rolled her eyes.

'Well, I don't know about that, but this cat certainly doesn't. I've never nibbled mouse in my life! For dinner this evening I had poached salmon, scallops and a little dollop of caviar. I also had some of the canapés that were being handed around at the party. It was all rather delicious! Far more tasty than a grubby mouse, I should think!'

She licked her lips at the thought of those delicious nibbles she'd helped herself to from the trays laid out in the kitchen at home.

'Now tell me what you were thinking, trying to cross that busy road when you are scarcely much bigger than a walnut!'

Winston took a few steps closer to the cat who smiled at him kindly. He was feeling less afraid now. The closer he got to his rescuer, the more he could see that she wasn't pretending. Her eyes twinkled with kindness that seemed absolutely genuine. She had silky, snowy fur and a diamond collar that glinted and gleamed in the light of a nearby lamp post.

'My name's Prudence,' said the cat. 'Lady Prudence Merryweather-Whiskerton the Third, if you want my full title. But most people call me Pru.' She eyed Winston with his grubby fur and tatty scarf. 'And you are?' If she'd been wearing spectacles, she would have been looking at him over the top of them.

Winston shyly introduced himself and for the second time that evening he found himself telling his tale about the

Important Mission to deliver his letter to Father Christmas, who was apparently right at this very moment in Fortesque's Department Store!

'But now I've lost the letter,' he said, sighing. 'So whoever wrote it isn't going to have a very happy Christmas at all, and it'll be all my fault.'

Pru listened to Winston. Then she looked around, squinting as she peered across the street.

'I say,' she said, 'that wouldn't be it over there, would it? Stuck to that traffic light?'

Winston had to stand on tiptoes to see where Pru was pointing.

He couldn't believe it – there was the letter! Still stuck exactly where it had been all along. He'd lost sight of it when he was being spun around in circles and almost flattened. The envelope was looking a bit damp and tatty now and the writing on the front seemed a tiny bit smudged.

'Yes! That's it!' cried Winston excitedly.

Pru lowered herself down on to the snow.

'Come on!' she said, slightly bossily. 'Hop on my back, and we'll go and fetch it!'

Winston wasn't sure. He hesitated, looking a bit nervous.

'For goodness' sake, you aren't a salmon so I'm not going to eat you!' said Pru.

Winston laughed and carefully

clambered up on to the shoulders of his strange new friend. Her fur was thick and soft and as Winston sank into it he felt warm for the first time that evening.

Once he was settled, Pru waited for a suitable gap in the traffic before bounding across the street in a few easy pounces.

She leaped up and retrieved Winston's letter with her mouth and flung it over her shoulder for her passenger to catch.

'And now,' she said grandly, 'time for us to deliver it to Fortesque's!'

'You know where it is?' asked Winston.

Pru laughed. 'Know it? Why, everything I own comes from there. It's the only place in town my people shop.

They had my collar made there by the head jeweller. You'll get there much quicker if I take you. I know where I'm going – and, besides, I doubt you can get anywhere quickly with such tiny feet!'

Winston laughed and held on tight as she elegantly trotted down the street. He couldn't believe that he was riding on the back of a cat.

What a strange night it had turned into!

PURVEYORS OF
FINE GOODS
SINCE 1847

Travelling through the city at night on the back of a large white cat was something Winston had never ever imagined himself doing. Now that he was actually doing it he couldn't believe how exciting and exhilarating it was!

With the rescued (and only slightly soggy) letter once again tucked under his arm, Winston gripped on tightly to his new feline friend and whizzed through the city at a terrific speed.

Now that he didn't have to make sure he wasn't about to be stepped on by a giant shoe every few seconds, Winston was able to look around and find out what the city was really like on Christmas Eve.

The first thing he noticed, or rather his tummy noticed, was the smell of glorious food everywhere. Christmas Eve parties were in full swing, and the delicious wafts of food billowing out from hotel and restaurant kitchens made Winston's belly grumble like a beast. There were roast chestnut sellers on nearly every corner and the lovely heat from the braziers and the yummy nutty smell of the chestnuts was almost too much for Winston. He imagined leaping off Pru's back and having an impromptu winter picnic on the side of the road, gobbling up as many chestnuts as he could before he fell over with a big full belly. Once he'd delivered his letter to Father Christmas he might be able to sneak back to one of the sellers and see if anyone had dropped any nuts on the ground.

They zipped past an enormous Christmas tree that was standing in a small square surrounded on three sides by very tall, elegant houses. The tree was bedecked and bejewelled with hundreds

of baubles and glittering lights.
On a rink in front of the tree
lots of people all wrapped
up in woolly scarves and
hats and mittens were
whizzing about on
ice skates having
what looked like
a marvellous
time.

Winston wasn't sure he'd like ice skating. It was hard enough for such a tiny mouse to stand upright on snow – let alone on a sheet of ice! But it was wonderful to watch everyone having fun.

As they continued on their journey Pru and Winston came across more shops, restaurants and delicious smells, and Winston turned to listen to more lovely singing coming from nearby.

Pru suddenly swerved off the main road and dashed around a corner. She continued along for a short while before coming to a stop.

'There we are, young man,' she said, very pleased with herself. 'Fortesque's Department Store: Purveyors of Fine Goods since 1847!'

Winston looked up at the building, and his mouth dropped open. It was the fanciest, most extraordinary building Winston had ever seen.

It was covered in windows – large ones on the bottom floor, with smart claret-coloured canopies above them and smaller ones on the floors above. The building's grand and ornate facade seemed to shimmer and sparkle so the entire place shone brightly, like a pirate's treasure chest.

'It's beautiful!' Winston gasped. 'And Father Christmas is in there?'

'Well, that's what you told me!' said Pru. 'We'll head to the main doors over there and we can nip into the shop. It'll be easy. I expect the staff will know who I am because my people are always in there and talk about me non-stop,' she said. 'Now let's get that letter of yours delivered.'

Winston nodded and held on tightly

to Pru's fur as she skipped nimbly across the street and headed for the beautifully polished front doors of the building.

'Here we go!' said Pru as they trotted towards the entrance. 'It will be easy as p—'

But she didn't finish her sentence because right at that very moment she walked straight into the legs of a man who had appeared out of the shadows.

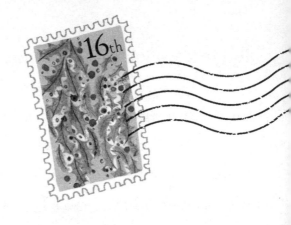

TEAMWORK

'And where do you think you're going?' said the man sternly. He glared at Pru from behind thick round spectacles. On his jacket a badge saying 'SECURITY' glinted in the moonlight.

'Hide!' hissed Pru.

Winston slid down from her back and hung upside down, clinging to the fur on her belly. Pru covered her surprise expertly and began to purr loudly, weaving in and around the man's legs and rubbing her shoulders up against the door. The security guard softened.

'What do you want to be going into this big shop for on Christmas Eve?' he said, smiling and bending down to tickle her ears with a thickly gloved hand. 'It's locked up tight for the holidays now. I just double-checked all the doors myself.'

He jangled a big set of keys cheerfully.

'Now, go on – I think you should head back home. Your people will be wondering where you are! Go on. That's it – shoo!' And very gently he guided Pru away so he could finish doing his final check of the front door and head home for Christmas.

Pru purred again and made a great show of walking nonchalantly down the road with her bushy tail swishing very casually behind her.

When they were a safe distance away, Winston scrambled on to her back again.

'What are we going to do now?' he squeaked in alarm. 'That man said the whole place is all locked up for the holidays.'

'We'll think of something,' said Pru.

Winston suddenly squeaked, 'Wait!

I can smell something!' He gingerly stood up on Pru's back and sniffed the night air. Yes! There was definitely something – his whiskers were wobbling, so Winston knew it must be important. What was it? He sniffed again. It smelt of nice things – flowers, soap, cookies, candy canes and lots of other rich and delicious aromas. It all seemed to be coming from inside the department store. But where was the smell escaping from? Was there a window open? Winston let his nose twitch and sniff until it found exactly the direction they needed to go.

'Down there!' he cried. And he pointed at a very dark alley. It wasn't appealing to go down such a forbidding passage but Pru and Winston both knew that their mystery letter-writer depended on them.

Pru picked her way down the passage. She could smell something now too. Eventually Winston told her to stop. He carefully slid down her silky fur and landed on the snowy ground.

'Here!' he said. 'The smells are coming from here!' He pushed his way forward and revealed an air vent only a few bricks up from the floor. 'I think this is a way we could get in! We can follow the smell through here until we get into the shop and then we can find our way to Father Christmas. Hopefully he won't have gone far!' Winston assessed the situation. 'We need to get that grille off,' he said. 'I can't squeeze in through those tiny gaps.'

Pru agreed. She reached a paw out and tapped the air vent experimentally. Both she and Winston jumped as it made an unexpected rattling noise.

'It's loose!' whispered Pru.

'Can you get it off?' asked Winston, watching with interest.

'I'm not sure,' said Pru. 'What we really need is something to undo these screws with.' She stopped rattling the grille and had a good look at it up close. 'I wonder . . .'

There was a flash from one of her paws as a claw suddenly appeared.

Winston gasped. It looked so sharp and shiny in the shadowy moonlight. He leaped backwards away from it.

'Oh, don't be such a silly sausage!'

Pru said. 'I'm going to see if I can use my claw as a screwdriver.' She delicately turned the loose screw, and eventually it clattered out of its hole and fell on to the snowy ground.

'HURRAH!' Winston hooted. 'Can you do the other ones? Then we can get to Father Christmas.'

Pru tried her hardest on all the other screws but they were as tight as glue.

'It's no good,' she said. 'They won't budge!'

Winston sighed.

'But,' said Pru, 'if I pull the grille forward, you might just be able to squeeze behind it! The gap certainly looks about Winston-sized!'

Winston nodded and clambered up

Pru's back again. He sucked in his tummy and – PLOP! – he landed gracefully (ish) behind the grille.

'OH BRAVO, WINSTON!' purred Pru. 'Here's the letter.' She carefully slid the envelope through the gap to him. 'Well done, little chap!' she said. 'That was excellent teamwork. You'd better get a move on though – you don't want Father Christmas leaving without you!'

'Aren't you coming with me?' he said.

Pru smiled. 'I'd love to, but I can't squeeze in there with you. My bottom's much too big! I'm afraid you'll have to do this next bit on your own.'

In the distance church bells chimed the passing of another hour.

'Goodness!' cried Pru. 'I had no idea it was so late! I'd better get back to my people! They get into a dreadful state when they can't find me.'

'Thank you, Pru,' said Winston. 'You are the nicest cat I've ever met!'

'And you are the nicest mouse,' she replied. 'Now hurry along! You've got a letter to deliver!'

Winston set his whiskers at a very determined angle. Waving over his shoulder at Pru, he set off down the dark tunnel into the shop. Pru watched him until she couldn't see him any longer before trotting off into the night.

DILLY-DALLYING

Winston edged his way tentatively down the tunnel. He was feeling nervous again. Pru had been an unlikely friend but her company and help had been just what Winston had needed. Now he was all alone again and heading into the unknown world of the department store.

He thought about the security man from earlier and was worried that there might be others in the shop. Would they notice him? What would happen if they caught him? And would Father Christmas still be in the store?

The smells from the shop were getting stronger and stronger and it wasn't long before a dim light illuminated the way in front of him. After turning the corner he soon came to another grille. Luckily this one was much more generous than the one in the alleyway. After rolling up the envelope and posting it through the grille, Winston set about squeezing himself through. It wasn't easy but after a few minutes of sucking in his tummy, folding up his ears and huffing and wiggling he popped out of the tunnel like a cork from a bottle of champagne and went tumbling, tail over ears, across the floor. He picked himself up and scurried back to collect his precious letter. It was only after he had stopped and listened for any human footsteps – and not heard any approaching – that he allowed himself to breathe properly and look around.

He was in a vast room. Thick fluffy carpet stretched out as far as he could see. Around him on all sides were well-polished counters and, if Winston went on tiptoes and really stretched his nose high, he could just about see what was displayed on top of them in their shiny glass fronts.

There were hats of all colours and designs, gloves of all lengths and fabrics, silky scarves and smart handbags all lined up in rows.

As Winston padded along he gazed at it all in awe. The building itself was beautiful, with carved wooden columns holding up the high vaulted ceiling. Although the main lights were off, hundreds of pretty Christmas garlands of holly, with baubles, crackers and tiny parcels nestled amongst them, were strung along every surface, their fairy lights twinkling and sparkling, making the whole place look like

a glittering, magical grotto.

The smells Winston had sniffed outside were almost overwhelming now that he was inside the building. They tumbled over and around each other in his nose, and it made him feel a bit dizzy. He had to concentrate very hard to remember that Father Christmas was somewhere in the building – Winston didn't have time to be wandering about, dilly-dallying!

Hitching the letter securely under his arm, Winston marched off determinedly. He had absolutely no idea where he was meant to be going but he felt that if he just kept walking sooner or later he would find

something that would
tell him where he was
and where he might find
Father Christmas.

And he was (sort of) right.

After several minutes of
walking between the display
cabinets and mannequins
the room opened up into
a huge atrium. Winston
craned his neck and looked up
and around him. Enormous richly
carved banisters and thickly carpeted
staircases wound their way up and around
the space leading the customers to the
treasures that were on sale on the other
five floors. At the top, the building
was finished off by a great

glass dome from which hung a gigantic crystal chandelier.

A large Christmas tree, lit up and decorated with ribbons and jewels, stood in the middle of the room. Winston spun around taking it all in.

Five floors! he thought, and he felt his ears droop. How would he be able to search for Father Christmas quickly across five floors? Just the thought of climbing the endless staircases on his tiny paws made Winston feel exhausted before he had even started!

He took a deep breath. 'Come on now, Winston!' he told himself. 'We're almost there!'

Forcing his ears to stop drooping, Winston decided that the best plan would be to search each floor in turn until he found Father Christmas.

He set off again but he hadn't got very far when a delicious smell wafted from somewhere nearby. He had smelt some food from outside in the alleyway but the scent was now so strong that it stopped him completely in his tracks. His little pink nose twitched as wafts of cookies and candy canes, pies and cheeses, fresh bread and party food all swirled around him. His stomach growled loudly like a lion. Winston's feet suddenly turned from the direction he had been travelling in and started marching him in the opposite direction towards the food.

'But the letter!' cried Winston. It was no use protesting. His nose, tummy

and feet were now in charge, and nothing was going to stop them from finding out where it was all coming from.

He found himself running back across the gentlemen's outfitters' department – past shiny leather brogues and tweed jackets and displays of silk ties of every colour fanned out behind a model peacock.

He whizzed by the cashmere scarves, beautiful coats and silk pyjamas. He swerved around a tower of hat boxes and through an archway before coming to a sudden halt.

Winston blinked in wonder. He couldn't believe what he was seeing in front of him!

STINKY AND THEREFORE TASTY

OOD! Food, everywhere!
Mountains of the stuff!
Wherever Winston looked
food danced in front of his eyes: glossy
fruit and vegetables in baskets; trays of
crisp pasties and pies; towering displays

of ornately iced cakes and golden-brown biscuits and sacks of exotic spices. A wall of wine bottles stood behind a beautiful counter. Canisters of teas with magical names were lined up like soldiers beside mounds of rich-smelling coffee beans.

There were mountains of nuts, castles of brightly filled jam jars and a long counter bursting with every kind of sweet imaginable. Everywhere hampers stamped with Fortesque's famous logo stood piled up in towers and arches, some with their lids open and all manner of delicious goods bursting out from inside.

There was also, realized Winston as his nose twitched wildly, CHEESE.

Somewhere in this enormous palace of food was wheel upon wheel of cheese.

And from the smell of it, it was some of the stinkiest, and therefore TASTIEST you could ever imagine.

Winston's stomach growled again. It was so loud it almost knocked him over. He realized that he was absolutely famished. He couldn't actually remember when he'd last eaten properly. Whatever it had been, it couldn't possibly have been as delicious as what was on offer in the hall full of grub.

Winston bit his lip and thought. He knew he shouldn't take anything – that would be stealing – but he was so hungry it was giving him tummy ache. The excitement of the evening so far had caught up with him and he felt his energy draining away. If he didn't eat something soon he doubted whether he'd be able to finish his mission. So Winston made a decision: he would just go and see if he could find where the cheese was and if he could find some tiny bits – crumbs really – he would eat them. He knew it was a bit naughty but the job he had to do was jolly important and he thought anyone else would do the same just so they were able to complete their mission.

So Winston hitched up the letter under his arm and took a step into the food hall.

And it was at exactly that moment someone threw a walnut at his head and shouted, 'OI!'

EDUARDO
FROMAGE

The walnut whistled through the gap between Winston's ears but the shout had almost made him leap out of his skin with fright! He looked around, panting, to see who or what was hollering at him.

It was a large rat. He was hanging over the top of one of the wicker hampers by the entrance to the food hall looking very cross indeed. He clambered out and made his way over to Winston who was still trying to get his breath back.

'Goodness me!' the rat was saying. 'Never have I seen anything like it in my life – approaching a food-preparation area looking like you've just rolled in a muddy ditch! Just think of the germs!' Then he shuddered from his whiskers to his tail and recoiled away from Winston as though he were made of fire.

'I'm sorry,' said Winston. 'Have I done something wrong? I was only going

to have a tiny bit of chee—'

'Wrong?' The rat snorted. 'You were about to go wandering amongst some of the finest foods available in the world and just look at you! You're filthy! Absolutely filthy!'

Winston looked down at himself. In the warm yellow glow of the food hall's Christmas lights, he had to admit that he did look very grubby indeed. He turned his paws over and was shocked to see that

their usual pinkness had disappeared under a thick layer of dirt. His ears drooped with embarrassment and, under the layer of grime, his cheeks flushed bright pink.

'I'm so sorry,' he squeaked. 'I'm just really hungry, and I've had quite a busy night.'

The rat sniffed rather haughtily but softened when he saw how little and floppy-eared and tired Winston looked.

'Not to worry, little chap!' he said, before drawing himself up proudly. 'My name, by the way, is Eduardo Fromage. I like to think of myself as the night manager here and as such I can't have any germs getting near the grub. It would be a terrible business. You've got to be shipshape and sparkling clean to go into the food hall. Like me! Look how shiny my fur is! And smell me! That's the most expensive cologne the store sells!'

Eduardo turned around slowly on the spot for Winston to admire his glossy fur and exquisitely curled whiskers – and to take in the rather strong smell of spicy perfume and soap.

'Now let's get you scrubbed up and fed!' Eduardo said kindly. 'What's your name, by the way?'

Winston told him.

'Marvellous!' said Eduardo. 'Well, you just follow me, and soon you'll be sparkling!'

Five minutes later Winston found himself on a gleaming white counter in another section of the department store. Instead of food this bit of the shop had all sorts of crystal bottles full of coloured liquids and little pots and boxes of powders and creams as far as the eye could see. There were lots of advertisements with pictures of glamorous men and women on them and the entire place smelt of roses and summer meadows and cleanliness. There were mirrors everywhere and Eduardo stopped every few seconds en route to admire himself in them. Winston got quite a start

when he saw his own reflection – he was a frightful state! No wonder Eduardo had thrown a walnut at him!

On the way Winston had tried to explain his Important Mission, and that – as lovely as a wash would be – he had to track down Father Christmas in the shop before he set off around the world on his sleigh. The trouble was Eduardo liked to natter. He nattered and nattered and nattered and Winston couldn't get a word in edgeways!

It turned out that Eduardo had lived in the department store all his life and no one (apart from the owner, Mr Fortesque, of course) knew the place better. When the shop was closed Eduardo spent his evenings wandering about the place making sure that everything was spick and span. Living in Fortesque's had given him quite a taste for the finer things in life. His office – as he called it – was a hamper lined inside with a silk scarf and lots of lavender-scented pillows.

Eduardo explained most of this as he was filling a small sink with water. When he was satisfied there was enough in the basin he said, 'Righty-ho, Winston! In you get!'

'In there?' asked Winston, peering over the side. His only other experience with water was puddles. He unwound his scarf from his neck and gingerly clambered down and found that the water was rather warm. He paddled around in it. It was quite fun and he giggled as the water splashed about between his toes.

Suddenly a great dollop of floral-smelling cream landed on his head. Eduardo was hard at work dragging over lots of different bottles of lotions and creams and was squirting them into the sink and all over Winston. He told Winston to give his fur a good scrub.

Winston was slightly dubious at first but he did as he was told and before long the water in the sink was murky and brown as all the dirt from the city streets came away. After a quick rinse Eduardo helped Winston out and handed him a flannel. Winston finally emerged gleaming white, his fur almost sparkling.

'Nice and clean!' announced Eduardo. 'No germs and you look much better. I think it's time we had a little something to eat.'

Winston didn't say anything. He didn't have to – his tummy grumbled very loudly in excitement as he followed Eduardo back to the food hall towards all that delicious-smelling grub!

A NIGHT-TIME FEAST

ack in the food hall Eduardo and Winston decided to make a late-night picnic. They washed their paws again at one of the sinks behind the food counters before Eduardo expertly started to put together a menu. It was Winston's job to follow him around and carry the increasingly tall and wobbly tower of food they were selecting. Their feast mainly consisted of cheese – lots and lots of different sorts. There was soft squidgy cheese, hard cheese, cheese with herbs in it and cheese with holes so big that Winston could put his head through them.

'I suppose,' said Eduardo, 'we oughtn't to have only cheese . . .' And he popped a couple of crackers on the top of the tower of cheeses then added a sliver of vegetable pie, some chunks of apple, several chocolate coins and a large gingerbread biscuit iced with a snowflake design for pudding.

'Marvellous!' cried Eduardo, thrilled with his selections. 'Shall we eat?'

Winston thought he'd never ask!

The two new friends decided to set out their feast under the Christmas tree in the main hall. Eduardo had found a crisp white linen napkin and they spread it out on the floor, piling the food on top of it. Despite the vast size of the department store entrance hall it felt so cosy to be sitting under the tree in the gentle glow of the twinkling tree lights.

Winston sat down and helped himself to a large chunk of the stinkiest cheese they had found. He was just about to put as much of it in his mouth as would fit (and maybe a bit more!) when Eduardo turned to him.

'Now, forgive me, young chap,' he said, 'but I don't believe you told me what you are doing in my store on Christmas

Eve. Shouldn't you be tucked up asleep at home?'

Winston lowered his giant pawful of cheese and explained sadly that he didn't actually have a home.

'Ah . . . I see,' said Eduardo, taking a chomp out of a buttery cracker. 'Well, I'm sure it wouldn't be a problem for you to live here. There's plenty of space, and it's jolly nice to have some company.

Usually I'm just snoozing in my hamper or snooping on the letters in the post room. Terribly interesting!'

Letters! Post! OH, CRUMBS! Winston suddenly remembered what he was meant to be doing! The letter! He'd been so busy with his bath and the picnic that he had forgotten his Important Job. He looked around – the letter to Father Christmas was nowhere to be seen. A shiver of dread ran right to the tip of his tail. He hopped up on to his feet and began pacing back and forth.

'Oh, bother! Bother! Bother! I've lost it! It's gone!' he squeaked.

'Whatever's the matter?' asked Eduardo. 'What's gone?'

'My letter! Well, not MY letter, but

the one I was carrying. It was a big envelope and I had it with me and now I don't!'

'Oh!' cried Eduardo, catching on. 'That tatty piece of paper? I tidied that away into my office before we went to get you all washed up before supper.'

Winston gasped. 'I need to get it back!'

Quickly the two new friends piled their picnic up in the napkin and Eduardo slung it over his shoulder. They raced back to Eduardo's hamper. On the way, Winston twittered and squeaked his way through explaining his Very Important Mission. Eduardo couldn't believe what he was hearing!

When they got there, Eduardo handed the letter back to Winston.

'Now I can deliver it to Father Christmas!' said Winston, relieved. 'I hope he's still here!'

Eduardo's brow wrinkled. 'Here?' he said. 'In Fortesque's?'

'Yes!' said Winston. 'I saw an advert: "Visit him in store today!"'

Eduardo stopped, clambering back out of his hamper house. He looked crestfallen.

'Oh dear, oh dear,' he said sadly. 'Come with me, Winston. I need to show you something very important . . .'

CLOCKWORK

Winston couldn't believe it.

'Clockwork?' he whispered. 'It's not the real Father Christmas at all but a clockwork one?'

He was now standing in one of the enormous windows of Fortesque's looking at the extraordinary scene in front of him. Everything was set up as if they were in Father Christmas's workshop at the North Pole. In the middle of the display stood Father Christmas but he wasn't a real person at all. He was a lovely (and probably very expensive) model – but a model nevertheless.

'I'm afraid so,' said Eduardo sadly. 'We always have lovely Christmas window displays here at the store, but this is the biggest and most extravagant we've ever had. It's taken almost a whole year to plan and make. We've had crowds of people standing outside looking at it and people have travelled for miles to see it. Watch . . .' Eduardo disappeared behind one of the painted background panels and carefully flicked a number of switches that were hidden away out of sight.

The window suddenly came to life!
Lights flickered on and a curtain of
pretend snow began to fall behind
an artificial window at the back
of the workshop. Christmas
music started to play and all
around Winston things
sprang into motion –
train sets chugged

around the scene puffing out smoke, toy aeroplanes swooped and looped overhead, rows of teddy bears waved their fluffy paws and dolls danced in circles.

Clockwork elves dashed about on hidden tracks, each carrying parcels or toys or bunches of carrots for a reindeer whose head appeared every so often through the workshop door.

And then there was Father Christmas himself, surrounded by sacks overflowing with gifts, checking a long, scrolling list in his hand, then waving to the imaginary crowds outside. His eyebrows waggled and he smiled and every so often his big belly would jiggle with glee at the scene around him.

It really was wonderful but Winston couldn't enjoy any of it. He felt so wretched and sad. He'd tried so hard to deliver his letter but he'd let his hungry tummy distract him. He should have known that the REAL

Father Christmas wouldn't have time to be standing around in shops on Christmas Eve. And now it was too late to get the envelope to the North Pole.

Winston slumped against Father Christmas's boots and covered his face with his ears. 'Whoever wrote that letter isn't going to get anything tomorrow morning and it's all my fault!' he groaned.

Eduardo watched Winston and felt helpless. If only there was some way he could help his young friend out. He looked about him for any inspiration, suspecting that he wouldn't find any, but hoping nevertheless.

Suddenly his eyes fell on something that planted the seed of an idea in his mind.

'All might not be lost, Winston!' he said slowly.

'But it is already,' said Winston sadly. 'I'll never get to the North Pole now.'

Eduardo grinned. 'I think you might!'

'How?' said Winston, sitting up.

Eduardo pointed to one of the toy planes that was busy loop-the-looping above their heads and said, 'You're going to fly!'

THE GREAT
FLYING MOUSE

'ME?' cried Winston. 'FLY?'

'Yes,' said Eduardo, as if it was a perfectly ordinary everyday thing for a mouse to take to the skies. 'It'll be easy! Look – there's a Winston-sized seat behind the controls of that plane. We'll take it up to the roof and you can set off from there. You'll be at the North Pole in no time at all — you might even meet Father Christmas's sleigh on the way!'

Winston wasn't in the slightest bit sure about any of this. It was dangerous enough for a little mouse like him just walking about the city; he didn't dare to imagine what it might be like to fly above one! And how would he ever know which way the North Pole was? He didn't have a map.

'Don't worry!' said Eduardo, as if reading Winston's mind. 'Look for the brightest star in the sky and that's the North Star. Just follow that and you'll know you are going the right way.'

Winston still wasn't convinced but then he looked at the envelope he'd been carrying all evening. *Everyone deserves a happy Christmas*, he thought to himself.

He HAD to fly that plane to the North Pole and complete his mission – no matter how scary it was. He stuck out his chin and nodded.

'I'll do it!' he said.

'OH, BRAVO!' hooted Eduardo, beaming. 'We haven't a moment to lose!'

They clambered up the model Father Christmas and, standing on his head, unhooked the toy plane from the ceiling and carefully lowered it to the ground.

'Right!' Eduardo puffed, when they were safely back on the floor. 'Now we just need to get it up to the roof.'

Winston thought of all the hundreds

of steps that wound up and around the five storeys from the entrance hall and he groaned. 'It's going to take us all night to get up the stairs with this! It's quite heavy.'

'Oh, we aren't going to take the stairs. We'll whizz up to the roof in the elevator!' said Eduardo. 'Follow me!'

Winston hadn't a clue what an elevator was but he had no choice other than to help Eduardo with the plane and tag along with him. He walked as briskly as he could towards a row of shiny brass doors set in a row on a nearby wall. Potted palm plants separated them and Eduardo scampered up one to press a neat little button set into the wall.

The ground immediately began to tremble and Winston felt afraid. What was happening? He glanced at Eduardo. He was back beside Winston now and was cheerfully waiting and whistling a jolly Christmas tune.

The trembling stopped and one set of doors opened, revealing a velvet-lined and gold-trimmed elevator. Eduardo hurried Winston and the plane inside. He clambered up the velvet wall coverings and pressed a little button that was hidden behind a small plate underneath rows of other larger buttons. The entire thing started to shake and shudder as it began to whoosh upwards.

'That's a secret button for getting straight to the roof,' said Eduardo proudly. 'Only important staff like me know about it . . .'

Winston would never forget the short journey in the elevator. He didn't know what was up or down, he was jostled all about and he tumbled over several times. It was a relief when they came to a stop and the doors flew open with a smart little ding of a bell.

They dragged the plane out on to the roof and looked about in silence. The weather had taken a turn for the worse while Winston had been inside the department store. A fearful wind roared and howled and thick curtains of snow swirled around him making it very difficult to see.

Winston gulped. His fur was prickling with nerves. If he squinted, he could just make out the other buildings of the city stretching out all around him. He was very high up and he could hear the traffic purring far below.

'We'll need a good runway for you to take off from!' shouted Eduardo over the wind. He pointed to a raised buttress at the back of the building. It was only a foot or so off the ground and by pushing and shoving and heaving and pulling they got the plane up on top of it.

The tiny plane rocked wildly. The propeller started to spin. Winston clambered into the cockpit. There was another seat behind him but it was too small for Eduardo to join him.

'You'll have to stay here!' shouted Winston over the noise. 'Thank you for all your help!'

Eduardo patted Winston kindly on the paw. 'You are welcome here at Fortesque's any time you like!'

Winston nestled down into his seat and gripped the controls tightly. Eduardo started to push the plane, slowly at first, and then faster and faster. The edge of the building came into view, and beyond it just seemed like a big black void with snow swirling like a whirlpool.

The propellor whirred.

Winston held his breath.

And, with a final shove, Eduardo pushed Winston and the plane over the edge of the roof.

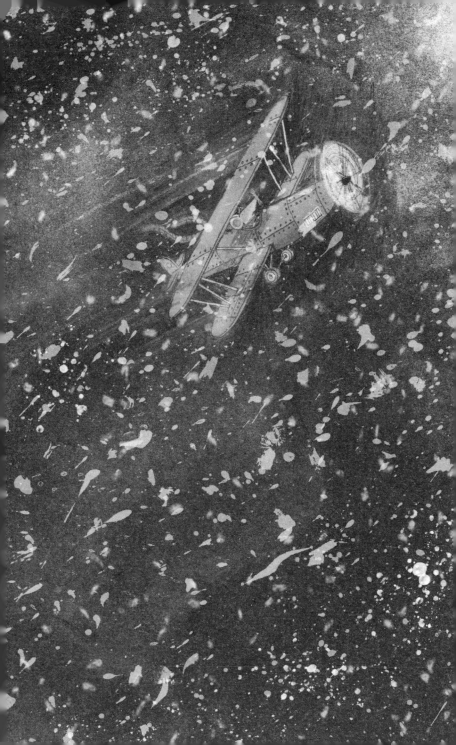

A LIGHT
IN THE SKY

He was actually flying! He quickly discovered that it was quite difficult to keep the plane going in the right direction. The wind really was dreadfully fierce and snow whirled around so he could barely see the front of the little aircraft.

'Follow the brightest star in the sky!' Winston told himself, remembering Eduardo's words.

But he didn't even know where the sky was! The snow storm became a full-blown blizzard and the plane was buffeted in all directions.

Winston shivered and concentrated on trying to keep hold of the letter. He kept looking for any flashes of bright light that could be the North Star.

As he was pulling the plane up out of quite a sharp dive he spotted a light in the sky. He blinked and tried to find it again.

Aha! There it was! It was some way off in the distance. A little bright red circle of light. What could that possibly be? Winston banked to the left, towards the strange glowing orb, but it disappeared into the thick white fog of the blizzard.

'Oh, great cheese and crackers!' exclaimed Winston.

All of a sudden the red glowing light was almost on top of him. He was heading straight for it! It was too late to avoid a collision! Winston grabbed hold of the letter with both paws and crouched as low as he could in his seat.

A confusion of fur and legs and antlers raced towards him. He closed his eyes tight.

CRASH!

The plane's tiny propellers snapped off and a wing was almost completely torn away. It spiralled downwards faster and faster. The wind whistled past Winston's ears and he carefully opened his eyes. Dark shapes were speeding towards him.

Buildings, he realised. Big ones. He was still above the city. The large, wide roof of a skyscraper was rushing towards him. Suddenly, Winston was thrown clear

from the plane and found himself falling
through the night sky before landing with
a wallop in a deep snow drift on the roof
of a tall building.

The last thing Winston heard before
everything went cold and white was the
sound of the tiny toy plane crashing and
splintering into pieces.

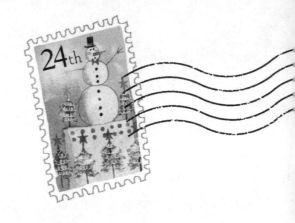

THE END

All was white and silent.

Minutes ticked by. Eventually Winston managed to open his eyes and a great buzzing and ringing sounded in his ears. He crawled out from under the snow. He had no idea where he was or even how far he'd travelled from Fortesque's.

'What am I going to do now?' he whispered to himself.

Everything seemed hopeless: the letter, Christmas, finding somewhere safe and warm for himself out of the storm. He stood as best he could in the wind and looked all around. He felt utterly lost and completely alone.

Across the great expanse of the rooftop where he had crash-landed, someone was moving about. He glimpsed a blur of red. He realized that this could be his only hope of getting down from this roof to safety. The snow whirled, and the figure disappeared into the whiteness. *Where did they go?* Winston wondered. He was so tired and achy now that he could barely stand. The figure in red swam into view. Winston looked again, trying to make out who it was. He gasped. It couldn't be!

'Wait!' cried Winston. 'WAIT!'

But his squeaks were snatched away by the wind.

He'd have to give chase, he thought, so he pitter-pattered across the roof as fast as his tiny feet could carry him waving the envelope above his head.

The snow was coming thick and fast, the wind was howling and everything was white and confusing. It was like being in a snow globe that was being madly shaken about.

'Wait!' Winston squeaked again. He couldn't walk another step. A blast of wind knocked him over and he landed on top of the envelope with a bump. He was too exhausted to get up again, so he just lay there shivering . . .

A few moments later, the figure appeared again out of the whiteness. He was small and round with a fluffy white beard and rosy red cheeks peeking out like two cherries on top of an ice cream. He was bundled up against the chill in a cheerful outfit. Winston opened one eye as wide as he could manage and smiled weakly.

'I knew I'd find you!' he squeaked.

Father Christmas cocked an ear. What was that? He'd heard a noise. It was a tiny and squeaky sort of a noise, but he'd definitely heard it. It sounded like a mouse. But what on earth would a mouse being doing up on a roof in this awful weather?

He looked around him and spotted what looked like the broken remains of a toy plane sticking out of a snow drift. Then he spotted something else. Lying on the ground almost completely covered in snow was the tiniest mouse he'd ever seen. And he seemed to be holding on to something very tightly.

Father Christmas gently picked Winston up and carefully placed him in his pocket for warmth. Then he looked with interest at the damp and crumpled piece of paper the little creature had been holding.

It was an envelope. And it was addressed to him! And inside, a letter from Oliver – the little boy who lived above the toy shop on Mistletoe Street.

Father Christmas scratched his head for a moment. He hadn't heard from Oliver this year. He'd thought that the boy had forgotten to write to him. But now he had his letter in his hand. Had it got lost in the post? Could that tiny little creature have been trying to deliver it? Surely not on a fearful night like this? It seemed unbelievable, yet here was a mouse on the roof holding the letter in his little paws.

'Extraordinary!' said Father Christmas, shaking his head in amazement.

He tucked Oliver's letter into his jacket for safety and carefully reached into his pocket. Winston had found a spare glove in there and had curled up inside it to keep warm so Father Christmas picked him up – glove and all – and looked at him.

'And what about you?' he said quietly as he stroked Winston's head.

'What would a brave little thing like you wish for at Christmas?'

Winston didn't say anything. He was fast asleep. He just snuggled deeper into his warm makeshift sleeping bag and snored loudly.

'I see . . .' said Father Christmas, and his eyes twinkled magically.

He looked up at the sky. The wind had stopped howling and the blizzard had calmed, so the snow was once again falling lazily on the city.

'I think I've got one extra little delivery to make before morning,' he said.

And he put Winston carefully back in his pocket, climbed into his sleigh and, with a flick of the reins, took off over the rooftops and up into the sky.

HOT BUTTERED TOAST

Even before he'd opened his eyes, Winston knew that something very strange and unusual had happened. The last thing he could remember was being outside in the freezing cold with the angry wind and snow roaring all around him. And he remembered being tired. Very tired indeed and freezing cold too – the sort of cold that makes you feel frozen from the inside out.

But that wasn't the case now at all. Winston was – he considered it for a moment – he was SNUGGLY. Really warm and cosy and, yes, very snuggly indeed. He sniffed. His whiskers wobbled with excitement. What was that lovely smell? It smelt like someone very nearby was cooking something very delicious. Where on earth was he?

He opened his eyes and looked around him and gasped. What had happened? He wasn't outside on the street in a hidey-hole which was where he woke up most mornings. He was in a bed! A perfect little mouse-sized bed with soft flannel sheets, a thick blanket and two great big plump pillows. There was even a little patchwork quilt keeping him toasty.

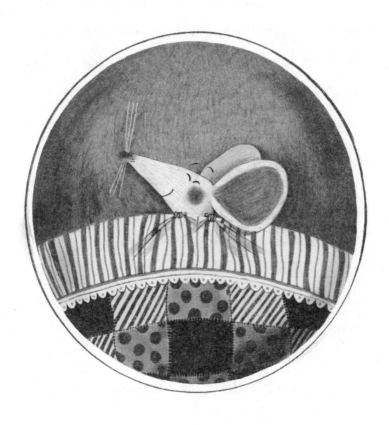

Winston wiggled his toes and looked around. He seemed to be in a little bedroom in a house where everything was just the right size for him. There were tiny books, a small armchair and – as Winston peeked over to look down the side of his bed – on the floor was a pair of tiny slippers that Winston knew, just from looking at them, would fit his feet perfectly.

What is this lovely place? he wondered.

A house made just for a mouse? Was he still asleep? Was he dreaming?

Then he heard a noise. A great stampede of thuds and whoops – of footsteps and voices. Human voices.

'Now be careful on the stairs, Oliver! What on earth has got you so giddy this morning?'

There were some very excited squeaking noises before Winston heard:

'What letter, Oliver?'

Oliver? thought Winston. *Who was Oliver?*

Just then there was a rattling noise. It sounded like someone was right outside his room. Winston burrowed down deep beneath his bed covers so only his eyes were peeking out over the top of his blanket. He couldn't believe what he was seeing! The entire far wall of his room swung open and a little boy's face appeared.

The little boy was in his pyjamas and his curly hair was sticking wildly up on end. His cheeks were bright pink and his eyes were sparkling with excitement.

'Mum! Dad!' he cried. 'Come and

see! In the doll's house – there's a mouse! A real mouse fast asleep in the attic!'

There followed a great commotion as more faces joined the little boy's to peer in at Winston. Two were grown-up faces, and the other was a smaller face. All belonged to humans in pyjamas and dressing gowns and everyone looked like they had jumped out of bed in a great hurry!

'Goodness!' said the grown-up face with a bristly moustache under its nose. 'There IS a mouse in the doll's house!'

'Father Christmas said in his letter that I would find a friend in the doll's house! And it's a mouse!' squeaked the little boy.

'What letter, Oliver?' said the other

grown-up face. This one didn't have a moustache, but had its hair up in a headscarf.

The other very small face didn't say anything. She was too busy sucking on the sleeve of her nightie.

The little boy quickly handed over a small sheet of paper. 'This letter!' he said, shivering with excitement. 'It's from Father Christmas! I found it in my stocking this morning – look!'

The two grown-ups read the letter and as they did their eyes grew bigger and bigger with astonishment.

Dear Oliver,

Thank you for your letter. I believe it had rather an exciting journey to get to me but the important thing is that it found me in the end.

I understand from your note that what you would like more than anything this Christmas is a friend – someone to go on adventures with.

If you go downstairs and peek in at the attic bedroom of that lovely doll's house you will find a little someone there waiting for you. He should be a very suitable friend for you. (He's really good at adventuring!) I should think he'll be fast asleep when you find him. He's had quite a tiring evening.

Take great care of each other. I look forward to reading about all your adventures together in your letter next Christmas. Although maybe pop it in the post a bit earlier next year!

With best Christmassy wishes,
Your friend,
Father Christmas

'Well I never, Oliver!' exclaimed the grown-up with the headscarf. 'A mouse!'

The little boy beamed.

'I think we'd all better go and get dressed and then our new friend here can join us in the kitchen for breakfast!' said the grown-up with the moustache. 'Do you think he'd like some hot buttered toast?'

'He does rather look like he could do with a good meal,' said the other grown-up, smiling.

Oliver told his new friend that he'd be back for him as soon as he was dressed (and had brushed his hair, one of the grown-ups added) and the whole family

scampered off to get ready for
the day.

When he was quite
alone, Winston sat up and
blinked. He wasn't a street
mouse any more. He had a
warm home and – if the lovely
smells were to be believed – a yummy
breakfast, lunch and dinner ahead of
him. He also had a friend called Oliver.
How extraordinary!

Something crinkled at the foot of
his bed and Winston scrambled about in
the blankets until he found what it was: a
stocking! A little mouse-sized striped
stocking and in it was a tiny letter written
in the smallest mouse-sized writing he'd
ever seen.

Dear Winston,

Thank you so much for delivering Oliver's letter to me.

I can only imagine what sort of an evening you had trying to deliver it. It must have been very exciting, but dangerous too.

What a kind and brave mouse you are. For such a tiny creature you have an enormous heart: one which understands that nobody should ever be left out or forgotten – especially at Christmas.

Happy Christmas, Winston. And enjoy your new home.

With love from
Father Christmas

Winston folded the letter carefully and held it very close to his chest. Then he snuggled back down under the blankets in his new bed in his new house in his new home and for the first time in his life he felt warm from the tip of his nose to the end of his tail.

And as he lay there he wondered what adventures tomorrow would bring.

Until next Christmas . . .

Hello!

I've always loved winter. All those frosty mornings and getting cosy after being outside in the cold. And when December arrives Christmas magic is in the air!

The busy bustling shops, the glitzy decorations, the waiting and then of course the big day itself!

I got the idea when I was helping my niece and nephews write their letters to Father Christmas and I wondered (with a shiver) what would happen if one of the letters got waylaid? Hopefully there would be some kind person (or in this case a mouse) to deliver it for us. And what adventures would they have?

Of course Christmas isn't just about the things you buy from the shops. I wanted to write a story about

A Christmas angel
I made aged 4!
(He's very old now!) →

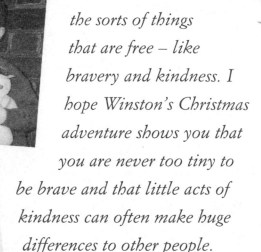

the sorts of things that are free – like bravery and kindness. I hope Winston's Christmas adventure shows you that you are never too tiny to be brave and that little acts of kindness can often make huge differences to other people.

I hope you've enjoyed this book and that you might come back to it next year and share it with other people in your family and with friends.

Have a very cosy Christmas and an adventurous New Year!

love from Alex
x

Me, aged two, playing in the snow!

ALEX T. SMITH is the creator of the bestselling *Claude* series and *Mr Penguin* series for early readers, as well as the much-loved *How Winston Delivered Christmas*, it's sequel *How Winston Came Home for Christmas*, and the witty retelling of *The Twelve Days of Christmas, or Grandma is Overly Generous*.

When not working, Alex enjoys doodling in his sketchbook, reading, people-watching and eavesdropping. He lives under the watchful eye of his small canine companions, who are a constant source of inspiration to him.